The kingdom of heaven is of the childlike,

of those who are easy to please,

who love and give pleasure.

ROBERT LOUIS STEVENSON

Illustrations copyright © Thomas Kinkade,
Media Arts Group, Inc., San Jose, CA

Text compilation copyright © 2000 by Tommy Nelson®,
a division of Thomas Nelson, Inc.

Published in Nashville, Tennessee, by Tommy Nelson®,
a division of Thomas Nelson, Inc.

Unless otherwise indicated, Scripture quotations are from the
International Children's Bible®, New Century Version®, copyright © 1986, 1988, 1999
by Tommy Nelson®, a division of Thomas Nelson, Inc. Used by permission.

Library of Congress Cataloging-in-Publication Data

A child's garden of prayers : a collection of classic prayers & timeless blessings:
featuring the artwork of Thomas Kinkade / compiled by Tama Fortner.
  p. cm.
  ISBN 0-8499-7603-0
  1. Children--Prayer-books and devotions--English. I. Kinkade, Thomas,
1958- II.   Fortner, Tama, 1969-

BV4870 .C45 2000
242'.8--dc21   00-041819

Printed in the United States of America
00 01 02 03 04 05 / OKP / 9 8 7 6 5 4 3 2 1

THOMAS  KINKADE

A
Child's Garden
OF PRAYERS

A COLLECTION OF
Classic Prayers & Timeless Blessings

Compiled by Tama Fortner

Tommy NELSON

Thomas Nelson, Inc.
Nashville

Teach a Little Child to Pray

Lord, teach a little child to pray,
    And then accept my prayer,
You hear all the words I say
    For You are everywhere.

A little sparrow cannot fall
    Unnoticed, Lord, by Thee;
And though I am so young and small
    You take good care of me.

Teach me to do the thing that's right,
    And when I sin, forgive;
And make it still my chief delight
    To serve You while I live.

JANE TAYLOR (Adapted)

"Lord, please teach us how to pray."

LUKE 11:1

Talking to God

God has entrusted you with one of His most precious creations—the soul of a child. He has loaned this soul to you for loving care and safekeeping, trusting that you will do all you can to ensure that this precious soul will one day be returned to Him.

God has also given both you and your child a most wonderful gift—the privilege of talking with Him through prayer. By following your example, your child will learn that God is a friend who is always there—to listen, to trust, and to praise.

As you share this book with your child, you are sharing prayers and blessings that have built a foundation of love and faith for generations, and you are also building the foundation for your child's own prayer life. Encourage your child to take the messages of these simple prayers and create prayers of his or her own. There is a space on pages 56–57 to record these prayers.

Prayer, in its simplest form, is talking to God, who is always eager to listen. Heads may be bowed or gazing up to heaven; eyes may be open or closed; bodies may be kneeling or standing. The only true requirement is a heart that is seeking God.

As the years pass by, your precious child will receive many gifts from you, but the greatest gift you can give is a love for God.

Let us pray, for God loves us;
Let us pray, for God hears us;
Let us pray, for God is our God,
And we are all His children.

UNKNOWN

For My Little One: Parents' Prayers

Thanks be to God for his gift
that is too wonderful to explain.

2 CORINTHIANS 9:15

Give me a little child to point the way
Over the strange, sweet path that leads to thee;
Give me a little voice to teach to pray;
Give me two shining eyes thy face to see.
The only crown I ask, dear Lord, to wear
Is this: that I may teach a little child.

UNKNOWN
"A Little Child"

Dear God,
Thank You for the gift of this tiny child.
Help me to show him Your love and Your greatness.
Help me to teach him the right way to live,
so that as he grows older
he will always follow You.
Amen.

[Based on Proverbs 22:6]
TAMA FORTNER

Every child born into the world is a new thought of God,

An ever-fresh and radiant possibility.

KATE DOUGLAS WIGGIN

Where did you come from, baby dear?

Out of the everywhere into here.

Where did you get your eyes so blue?

Out of the sky as I came through.

Where did you get this pearly ear?

God spoke and it came out to hear.

But how did you come to us, you dear?

God thought about you, and so I am here.

GEORGE MacDONALD

Train a child how to live the right way.
Then even when he is old,
he will still live that way.

PROVERBS 22:6

For My Parents: Children's Prayers

Dear Father in heaven,

Look down from above;

Bless Father and Mother

And all whom I love.

UNKNOWN

May the love of God our Father

Be in all our homes today:

May the love of the Lord Jesus

Keep our hearts and minds always:

May his loving Holy Spirit

Guide and bless the ones I love,

Father, mother, brothers, sisters,

Keep them safely in his love.

UNKNOWN

Children, obey your parents the way the Lord wants.
This is the right thing to do.

EPHESIANS 6:1–2

Bless, O Lord Jesus, my parents,
And all who love me and take care of me.
Make me loving to them,
Polite and obedient, helpful and kind.
Amen.
UNKNOWN

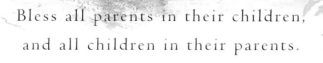

Bless all parents in their children,
and all children in their parents.

CHRISTINA ROSSETTI

For My Home

God makes our home a house of joy,
Where love and peace are given;
It is the dearest place on earth,
The nearest place to Heaven.

JOHN MARTIN
"Bless My Home"

Lord, behold our family
here assembled. We thank You
for this place in which we dwell,
for the love that unites us,
for the peace accorded us this day,
for the hope with which we expect
the morrow; for the health,
the work, the food,
and the bright skies
that make our lives delightful;
for our friends in all parts
of the earth. Amen.

ROBERT LOUIS STEVENSON

God bless the master of this house,

God bless the mistress too,

And all the little children

That round the table go.

UNKNOWN

God bless our home.

TRADITIONAL

God bless all those that I love;

God bless all those that love me;

God bless all those that love those that I love,

And all those that love those that love me.

From an old NEW ENGLAND SAMPLER

For Those I Love

Thank You, Lord, for giving me
A happy, caring family.
Thank You for the friends I meet;
And for neighbors down the street
But most of all, dear Lord above,
I thank You for Your precious love.

UNKNOWN

Dear Lord, I'd like to pray
for all the people that I love,
but who live far away.
Tonight with them my thoughts I share.
Please keep them in your loving care,
Each night and every day.

TRADITIONAL

God bless us every one!

CHARLES DICKENS

"Tiny Tim's Prayer"

If we love each other, God lives in us.

1 JOHN 4:12

For My Friends

Thank you for my friend next door,
And my friend across the street,
And please help me to be a friend
To everyone I meet.

UNKNOWN

When I wake up in the morning,
thank you, God, for being there.
When I come to school each day,
thank you, God, for being there.
When I am playing with my friends,
thank you, God, for being there.
And when I go to bed at night,
thank you, God, for being there.
UNKNOWN

Loving Father,
on this day
Make us happy
in our play,
Kind and helpful,
playing fair,
Letting others
have a share.
UNKNOWN

Heavenly Father, hear my prayer:
Night and day I'm in Your care;
Look upon me from above,
Bless the home I dearly love;
Bless the friends with whom I play,
Make us kinder day by day.
UNKNOWN

"Love each other.
You must love each other
as I have loved you."
JOHN 13:34

"Lord, you know that I love you."

JOHN 21:16

For Me

Two little eyes to look to God;

Two little ears to hear his word;

Two little feet to walk in his ways;

Two little lips to sing his praise;

Two little hands to do his will

And one little heart to love him still.

TRADITIONAL from Wales

Lord of the loving heart, may mine be loving too,
Lord of the gentle hands, may mine be gentle too.
Lord of the willing feet, may mine be willing too,
So I may grow more like you
In all I say and do.

UNKNOWN

All for You, dear God.
 Everything I do,
 Or think,
 Or say
 The whole day long.
Help me to be good.
UNKNOWN

Lord, teach me all that I should know;
In grace and wisdom I may grow;
The more I learn to do Your will,
The better may I love You still.
 ISAAC WATTS (Adapted)

Please give me what I ask, dear Lord,
If you'd be glad about it.
But if you think it's not for me,
Please help me do without it.
TRADITIONAL

Lord, teach me what you want me to do.
PSALM 86:11

I will praise you, Lord, with all my heart.
I will tell all the miracles you have done.

PSALM 9:1

For Your Praise, God

North and South and East and West,
May your holy name be blessed;
Everywhere beneath the sun,
As in heaven, your will be done.

WILLIAM CANTON (Adapted)

Dear God,

My mommy and daddy

have told me so much about You.

They have told me about all the mighty things

You have done and about Your many miracles.

They tell me how amazing You are,

and they teach me songs about Your great goodness.

I am going to tell all my friends about You,

because You are so wonderful!

Amen.

[Based on Psalm 145:4–7]

TAMA FORTNER

O Father of goodness,
We thank you each one
For happiness, healthiness,
Friendship and fun,
For good things we think of
And good things we do,
And all that is beautiful,
Loving and true.

PRAYER FROM FRANCE

The Twenty-Third Psalm

The LORD is my shepherd;

    I shall not want.

He maketh me to lie down in green pastures:

    he leadeth me beside the still waters.

He restoreth my soul:

    he leadeth me in the paths of righteousness

    for his name's sake.

Yea, though I walk through the valley

    of the shadow of death,

    I will fear no evil;

    for thou art with me;

    thy rod and thy staff they comfort me.

Thou preparest a table before me

    in the presence of mine enemies:

    thou anointest my head with oil;

    my cup runneth over.

Surely goodness and mercy shall follow me

    all the days of my life:

    and I will dwell in the house

    of the LORD for ever.

KING JAMES VERSION OF THE BIBLE

Dear God,

You are my shepherd.
You give me everything I need.
You give me rest and peace.
You give me new strength,
and you lead me on paths that are right.

Even if I walk through the darkness,
I will not be afraid because I know
that you are always with me.

You prepare a meal for me
in front of my enemies.
You pour oil on my head.
You give me more than I can hold.

I know that your goodness and love
will be with me all my life.
And I will live in the house
of the Lord forever.

[Based on Psalm 23]
TAMA FORTNER

Obey the Lord your God.
Then all these blessings will come and stay with you.
DEUTERONOMY 28:2

For My Blessings

Thanks to you, kind Father
For my daily bread,
For my home and playthings,
For my cozy bed.

Mother, father, dear ones—
Bless them while I pray:
May I try to help them,
Cheerfully obey.

CHARLES HEALING

All good gifts around us
Are sent from heaven above;
Then thank the Lord,
    O thank the Lord,
For all his love.

MATTHIAS CLAUDIUS

The Lord is good to me,
    and so I thank the Lord.
For giving me the things I need:
    the sun, the rain, and the apple seed!
The Lord is good to me.

TRADITIONAL

If you have plenty, be not greedy,
But share it with the poor and needy:
If you have a little, take good care
To give the little birds a share.

TRADITIONAL

For Making Me

God made the sun
  And God made the tree,
God made the mountains
  And God made me.

I thank you, O God,
  For the sun and the tree,
For making the mountains
  And for making me.

LEAH GALE
"A Birthday Grace"

You made my whole being. You formed me in my mother's body.
I praise you because you made me in an amazing and wonderful way.
What you have done is wonderful. I know this very well.

PSALM 139:13–14

God made the world so broad and grand,
Filled with blessings from His hand.
He made the sky so high and blue,
And all the little children too!
UNKNOWN

He prays best, who loves best
All things both great and small;
For the dear God who loves us,
He made and loves us all.
SAMUEL TAYLOR COLERIDGE
(Adapted)

This is the day that the Lord has made.
Let us rejoice and be glad today!

PSALM 118:24

For the World

O God,

You spoke and the sky appeared.

You breathed and stars filled the sky.

You made the oceans and the seas,

and you filled all the earth with your love.

Thank you, God, for this wonderful world. Amen.

[Based on Psalm 33:5–9]

TAMA FORTNER

Thank you for the world so sweet,
Thank you for the food we eat.
Thank you for the birds that sing,
Thank you, God, for everything!

EDITH RUTTER LEATHAM

Dear God in Paradise

Look upon our sowing:

Bless the little gardens

And the green things growing.

UNKNOWN

O Lord,
creator of all the world,
all living things
bless and praise you.

TRADITIONAL JEWISH PRAYER

Little drops of water,
Little grains of sand,
Make the mighty ocean
And the beautiful land.

Little deeds of kindness,
Little words of love,
Help to make earth happy,
Like the heavens above.

JULIA A. CARNEY
"Little Drops of Water" (Excerpt)

All Things Bright and Beautiful

All things bright and beautiful,
All creatures great and small,
All things wise and wonderful,
The Lord God made them all.

Each little flower that opens,
Each little bird that sings,
He made their glowing colors,
He made their tiny wings.

The tall trees in the greenwood,
The meadows where we play,
The rushes by the water
We gather every day—

He gave us eyes to see them,
And lips that we might tell
How great is God Almighty,
Who has made all things well!

CECIL FRANCES ALEXANDER

For the Animals

God bless the field and bless the furrow,
Stream and branch and rabbit burrow,

Bless the sun and bless the sleet,
Bless the lane and bless the street,

Bless the minnow, bless the whale,
Bless the rainbow and the hail,

Bless the nest and bless the leaf,
Bless the righteous and the thief,

Bless the wing and bless the fin,
Bless the air I travel in,

Bless the earth and bless the sea,
God bless you and God bless me.

AN ENGLISH PRAYER (Excerpt)

O Lord Jesus Christ, . . .
help us to be very kind to all animals and our pets.
May we remember that you will one day
ask us if we have been good to them.
Bless us as we take care of them; for your sake.
Amen.

UNKNOWN

The lark's on the wing;
The snail's on the thorn:
God's in His Heaven—
All's right with the world!
ROBERT BROWNING

Hurt no living thing:
Ladybird, nor butterfly,
Nor moth with dusty wing,
Nor cricket chirping cheerily,
Nor grasshopper so light of leap,
Nor dancing gnat, nor beetle fat,
Nor harmless worm that creep.
CHRISTINA ROSSETTI

I hope my words and thoughts please you.
PSALM 19:14

For Others

Lord, teach me to love Your children

everywhere, because

You are their Father and mine.

Amen.

UNKNOWN (Adapted)

Dear Lord, teach me to be generous;
To give and not to count the cost,
To work and not to seek for any reward,
Save that of knowing that I do your will.
ST. IGNATIUS LOYOLA

May God give us grateful hearts

And keep us mindful

Of the needs of others.

UNKNOWN

*"Be careful. Don't think these little children are worth nothing.
I tell you that they have angels in heaven
who are always with my Father in heaven."*
MATTHEW 18:10

For Serving You, Lord

Father, we thank you for the night,
And for the pleasant morning light;
For rest and food and loving care,
And all that makes the day so fair.

Help us to do the things we should,
To be to others kind and good;
In all we do at work or play
To grow more loving every day.

REBECCA J. WESTON

Bless me, O Lord, and let my food
strengthen me to serve You,
for Jesus Christ's sake.
Amen.

THE NEW ENGLAND PRIMER

Lord, make me an instrument of your peace.

Where there is hatred, let me sow love,

Where there is injury, pardon,

Where there is despair, hope,

Where there is darkness, light,

Where there is sadness, joy.

ST. FRANCIS OF ASSISI

Do all the good you can,

By all the means you can,

In all the ways you can,

In all the places you can,

At all the times you can,

To all the people you can,

As long as ever you can.

JOHN WESLEY

The Lord listens when I pray to him.

PSALM 4:3

For Jesus

Jesus, friend of little children,
   Be a friend to me;
Take my hand and ever keep me
   Close to thee.

Teach me how to grow in goodness
   Daily as I grow:
You have been a child, and surely
   You must know.

Never leave me nor desert me,
   Always be my friend,
I need you from life's beginning
   To its end.

WALTER J. MATHAMS (Adapted)

Be near me, Lord Jesus, I ask Thee to stay,

Close by me forever, and love me, I pray.

Bless all the dear children in Thy tender care,

And take us to heaven, to live with Thee there.

MARTIN LUTHER

Little Jesus, were You shy
Once, and just so small as I?
And what did it feel like to be
Out of Heaven, and just like me?
FRANCIS THOMPSON (Adapted)

For Jesus, My Savior

Savior, teach me, day by day,
Love's sweet lesson to obey;
Sweeter lesson cannot be,
Loving Him who first loved me.

JANE ELIZA LEESON

Gentle Jesus, meek and mild,
Look upon a little child;

Lamb of God, I look to Thee;
You shall my example be;

You are gentle, meek and mild,
You were once a little child.

Let me above all fulfill
God my heavenly Father's will;

Loving Jesus, gentle Lamb,
In Your gracious hands I am,

Make me, Savior, what You are,
Live Yourself within my heart.

CHARLES WESLEY
"Lamb of God I Look to Thee"

Loving Shepherd of your sheep

Keep your lamb in safety, keep;

Nothing can your power withstand,

None can pluck me from your hand.

JANE ELIZA LEESON

For the Morning

For this new morning and its light,

Father, we thank You;

For rest and shelter of the night,

Father, we thank You;

For health and food, for love and friends,

For every gift your goodness sends,

We thank you, gracious Lord.

RALPH WALDO EMERSON

"United States" (Adapted)

My Father, for another night

Of quiet sleep and rest,

For all the joy of morning light,

Your holy name be blessed.

HENRY WILLIAM BAKER (Adapted)

Through the night your angels kept
Watch beside me while I slept;
Now the dark has gone away;
Thank you, Lord, for this new day.

WILLIAM CANTON (Adapted)

For My Play

It is good to praise the Lord,
to sing praises to God Most High.

PSALM 92:1

Now before I run to play,
  Let me not forget to pray
To God who kept me through the night
  And waked me with the morning light.

Help me, Lord, love Thee more
  than I ever loved before,
In my work and in my play,
  Be Thou with me through the day.

UNKNOWN

Lord, through this day,
In work and play,
Please bless each thing I do.
May I be honest, loving, kind,
Obedient unto you.

UNKNOWN

The moon shines bright,
The stars give light
Before the break of day;
God bless you all
Both great and small
And send you a joyful day.
TRADITIONAL

Be full of joy in the Lord always.
PHILIPPIANS 4:4

Depend on the Lord.
Trust him, and he will take care of you.

PSALM 37:5

For My Busy Day

Thank You for each happy day,

For fun, for friends, and work and play;

Thank You for Your loving care,

Here at home and everywhere.

UNKNOWN

Lord, you know how busy I must be this day.

If I forget you, please do not forget me.

SIR JACOB ASTLEY (Adapted)

Thank you, God, for this new day

In my school to work and play.

Please be with me all day long,

In every story, game and song.

May all the happy things we do

Make you, our Father, happy too.

UNKNOWN

For Our Food

God is great, and God is good.
Let us thank Him for our food.
By His hand we all are fed;
Thank you, Lord, for our daily bread.
TRADITIONAL

For rosy apples, juicy plums
And honey from the bees,
We thank you, heavenly Father God,
For such good gifts as these.
UNKNOWN

Our hands we fold,
And heads we bow,
For food and drink
We ask Thee now.
Amen.
UNKNOWN

It is very nice to think
The world is full of meat and drink,
With little children saying grace
In every Christian kind of place.
ROBERT LOUIS STEVENSON

For what we are about to receive,

May the Lord make us truly thankful.

Amen.

TRADITIONAL

Come, Lord Jesus, be our guest,

And may our meal by you be blessed.

MARTIN LUTHER (Adapted)

For the Evening

Jesus, tender Shepherd, hear me,
Bless your little lamb tonight;
Through the darkness please be near me,
Keep me safe till morning light.

All this day your hand has led me,
And I thank you for your care;
You have clothed me, warmed and fed me,
Listen to my evening prayer.

Let my sins be all forgiven;
Bless the friends I love so well;
Take me, when I die to heaven,
Happy there with you to dwell.

MARY L. DUNCAN

Now the day is over,
Night is drawing nigh,
Shadows of the evening
Steal across the sky.

Now the darkness gathers,
Stars begin to peep,
Birds and beasts and flowers
Soon will be asleep.

Jesus, give the weary
Calm and sweet repose;
With your tender blessings
May our eyelids close.

Through the long night watches,
May your angels spread
Their white wings above me,
Watching round my bed.

When the morning wakens,
Then may I arise
Pure, and fresh, and sinless
In your holy eyes.

SABINE BARING-GOULD (Adapted)

My Nightly Blessing

O, holy Father, I thank You

for all the blessings of this day.

Forgive me for that which I have done wrong.

Bless me and keep me through the night,

For Jesus' sake.

Amen.

UNKNOWN

I can lie down and go to sleep.
And I will wake up again because the Lord protects me.

PSALM 3:5

For My Sleep

Now I lay me down to sleep.
I pray You, Lord, my soul to keep.
Your love be with me through the night
And wake me with the morning light.

TRADITIONAL

From ghoulies and ghosties,
Long-leggety beasties
And things that go bump in the night
Good Lord deliver us.

TRADITIONAL SCOTTISH PRAYER

Lord, when we have not any light,
And mothers are asleep,
Then through the stillness of the night
Your little children keep.

When shadows haunt the quiet room,
Help us to understand
That you are with us through the gloom,
To hold us by the hand.

ANNE MATHESON

Lord, You made the stars that brightly
Twinkle in the nighttime sky.
You made the clouds that float lightly
Above the trees and mountains high.
Lord, You know each one by number.
Your watchful eyes never slumber.
O Lord who made the stars above,
Watch me, guard me with Your love.

UNKNOWN

Lord, keep me safe this night,
Secure from all my fears;
May angels guard me while I sleep,
Till morning light appears.

JOHN LELAND (Adapted)

My Child's Prayers

Record your little one's prayers here.

The Lord's Prayer

Our Father in heaven,

we pray that your name will always be kept holy.

We pray that your kingdom will come.

We pray that what you want will be done,

here on earth as it is in heaven.

Give us the food we need for each day.

Forgive the sins we have done,

just as we have forgiven those who did wrong to us.

Do not cause us to be tested;

but save us from the Evil One.

MATTHEW 6:9–13

Index of Paintings